Haysville West Middle School Library

The Freedom Tree

by
Cynthia Mercati

Haysville West Middle School Library

Perfection Learning®

Illustration: Sue F. Cornelison
Design: Tobi Cunningham

About the Author

Cynthia Mercati is a writer and a professional actress. She has written many plays for a children's theatre that tours and performs at various schools. She also appears in many of the plays herself.

Ms. Mercati loves reading about history and visiting historical places. When she writes a historical play or book, she wants her readers to feel as if they are actually living the story.

Ms. Mercati also loves baseball. Her favorite team is the Chicago White Sox. She grew up in Chicago, Illinois, but she now lives in Des Moines, Iowa. Ms. Mercati has two children and one dog.

Text © 2002 by Perfection Learning® Corporation.
All rights reserved. No part of this book may be reproduced, stored in a retrieval system, or transmitted in any form or by any means, electronic, mechanical, photocopying, recording, or otherwise, without prior permission of the publisher.
Printed in the United States of America.

For information, contact
Perfection Learning® Corporation
1000 North Second Avenue, P.O. Box 500
Logan, Iowa 51546-0500.
Phone: 1-800-831-4190 • Fax: 1-800-543-2745
Reinforced Library Binding ISBN-13: 978-0-7569-0298-8
Reinforced Library Binding ISBN-10: 0-7569-0298-3
Paperback ISBN-13: 978-0-7891-5520-7
Paperback ISBN-10: 0-7891-5520-6
4 5 6 7 8 9 PP 12 11 10 09 08 07
perfectionlearning.com

Contents

1. The Favor 5
2. Seeming and Being 11
3. The Prisoner 20
4. Gone Forever 29
5. Yankees 36
6. No Time to Lose 44
7. Not Alone 51
8. Strong in My Soul 59
9. An End and a Beginning 65
10. The Freedom Tree 70

1
The Favor

I reached the big oak tree first. Quickly I settled the books and paper around me. I couldn't wait to start teaching Keely. And I knew she was even more impatient to start learning.

But we couldn't let anyone know what we were up to. It was against the law to educate slaves. It wasn't just a law on our plantation. It was true everywhere in the South.

If anyone discovered that Keely could read and write, she'd be punished. And I might be sent to jail. The law said a white person could be sent to jail for teaching a slave.

But I was willing to take the chance for Keely. We'd known each other all our lives—13 years. In all that time, she'd never asked me for anything. She'd never even hinted for one of my old dresses or a hair ribbon.

But she had asked me for this. She'd asked me to teach her. I remembered that day clearly.

🙟 🙟 🙟 🙟 🙟

"I have something to ask you, Miss Caro," Keely whispered to me. She darted a quick look over her shoulder to make sure we were alone in the parlor.

"I want you to teach me letters," she said. "I want to write. And I want to read."

I had stared at her in surprise, brushing back a flyaway curl. "I didn't know you cared about reading and writing."

Keely bobbed her head up and down. "I do, Miss

Caro. I care a powerful lot. Ever since I heard you with that teaching lady. Remember? I'd fan you while you did your learning."

I did remember. My older brother, Tad, had been sent away to school. But Father had seen no use in sending me. I was just a girl. Instead he'd hired Miss Edwards to be my tutor.

Miss Edwards was from the North. She'd had a difficult time with our warm Georgia weather. So on hot days, Keely had been in the schoolroom with us. Her job was to wave a big fan made from a palmetto leaf.

"I'd listen to you read, Miss Caro," Keely said. "I'd see you writing down words. They looked like chicken scratches to me. I wanted to look at those marks and know what they meant."

Keely shook her head at the wonder of it all. Softly she went on, "When you and the teacher were gone, I'd pick up a book. I'd run my hands over the writing. I'd look at those pages. I'd stare so hard, my eyes would hurt. I thought that if only I could look hard enough, the marks would make some sense."

She smiled sadly. "But of course they never did."

Keely lifted her head and sat up straight. She folded her hands tightly against her apron. There was determination in every line of her thin body. I could hear it in the tone of her voice.

THE FREEDOM TREE

"I promised myself that someday I'd be able to read and write for real," Keely continued. "Everyone's so busy now. Everything's so mixed up. I thought it would be a good time to learn."

I knew what Keely meant. In 1861, our state of Georgia had left the Union. We'd joined the Confederate States of America. That had been almost two years ago. Since then, the South had been at war with the North.

My father and Tad had been gone for those two years. They were fighting the Yankees.

Mother was in charge of our plantation now. For the first time in her life, she had to do real work. Unfortunately, it was work she hadn't been trained for. She was barely managing. Every day was a struggle.

Mother had only Ellie to turn to for help and advice. Ellie was Keely's mother. She had been a house slave on my grandparents' plantation. When my mother had married, Ellie came with her as her personal maid.

Before the war, my mother's face had been as smooth as a young girl's. Now she looked nervous all the time. Worry lines framed her mouth. They crisscrossed her forehead. At night I could hear her pacing the floor. Sometimes she talked with Ellie about her problems.

The Favor

Every day Mother said, "If only Mr. Haverton were here. Or Tad. I'm just a woman. How can I be expected to keep things going?"

I felt bad for Mother. She was in a terrible state. But Keely was right. Everything was so topsy-turvy now. No one would notice us sneaking off.

Keely looked me straight in the eye. She spoke firmly. "I'm asking you to teach me words, Miss Caro. I'm asking you because you once said you loved me like a sister."

"It will be my pleasure to teach you, Keely," I said quickly. And I meant it. It would be a risk, but I was prepared to take it.

"We'll meet every night after supper," I told her. "I know you have some free time then. We'll meet by the big oak. The one where we used to play dolls. We'll start tonight."

Keely's eyes filled with tears. Her voice was full of feeling. "I can hardly believe it," she breathed. "I always hoped—I always dreamed—but I never thought it would happen."

Keely wiped her eyes on her apron. "Thank you, Miss Caro. Thank you!"

"I can't believe it either," I said. "All this time you've been wanting to read and write. And I never knew."

A small half-smile touched Keely's lips.

THE FREEDOM TREE

"Slaves get mighty good at hiding things, Miss Caro. Especially the things we really and truly feel."

Now I sat by the big oak waiting for Keely. I thought about what she'd said. I wondered what other feelings she might be hiding.

🌸 🌸 🌸 🌸 🌸

And I realized that for the first time in my life, I was hiding something too.

2
Seeming and Being

As we had planned, Keely and I met every night. I was happy to have something to think about besides the war. It was also an escape from my difficult days.

THE FREEDOM TREE

I'd been born at The Cedars. That's what we called our plantation. It was named for the two long lines of big cedar trees that ran from the road to the front door.

The Cedars was almost like a small country. We made or grew almost everything we needed.

Male slaves were trained to be cobblers and carpenters. They fixed our wagons and took care of our horses.

Kitchen slaves grew our vegetables in a big garden. They worked in the orchard. Some prepared our meals in the big kitchen.

House slaves cleaned our rooms. They mended and sewed our clothing.

Field slaves tended to the animals. They also planted and picked our cotton.

Ellie was training Keely to be my maid. I was glad she'd never have to work in the fields under a scorching sun.

The Cedars was built with no particular plan. Rooms were just added willy-nilly. There were lots of them now.

Purple flowers hung over the big porch where we sat on warm nights. Pink and white bushes stood soft against whitewashed brick. In spring and summer, the wide lawn shone emerald green.

Our cotton fields rolled on for miles. They'd been

planted in curves to keep the soil from washing down to the swampy river bottom. Pine forests rested at the edge of the fields.

My father always said that we grew the best cotton in the world in Georgia. And that the best cotton in Georgia was grown on The Cedars.

Father always planned that Tad would take over the plantation someday. There was never any thought that I would help run it.

"Southern girls get married and have families," Father always told me. "You leave that nonsense about teaching school or working in a factory to Yankee girls."

Mother always told me that Southern girls had to please their husbands. Especially Southern girls like me. I was the daughter of a rich planter. Someday I would marry another rich planter.

To be pleasing, I was taught to dance and play the piano. I could also speak a little French. French was the latest fashion.

Mother taught me to do needlepoint. Her work decorates The Cedars. Someday, she said, my needlework would hang on the walls of my own plantation.

I didn't dislike the things I was taught. Nor did I particularly like them. It wasn't up to me to like or dislike anything. I'd been taught to obey my parents in all things. And that's what I did.

THE FREEDOM TREE

My parents would plan my future—just like they'd planned my past. They would choose who I would marry and where I would live. My parents would decide all of those things. I never thought of questioning them.

It used to seem that my life would be very much like my mother's. But now I wasn't so sure. Because now the war had changed everything.

We all thought the War Between the States would be a quick one. When the South won the first battle at Bull Run, everyone had said, "One more victory and we'll win this war." No one said that now.

At first it didn't seem to matter that the South was outnumbered. Everyone had said, "One Southern soldier is worth three Yankees."

Now we knew the Yankees could fight just as hard as our men. The North had blocked our southern harbors with their ships. That meant nothing could be shipped into the South. We were completely bottled up.

We had no one to depend on but ourselves. We had to grow everything we ate. But so many plantations and farms had been destroyed by the Yankees. The ones that were left were struggling to produce enough to feed our people.

The commissary troop rode through the countryside every month. Their job was to collect food and livestock and whatever else the army needed. Chickens, horses, cattle, pigs—they had the right to take it all.

Mother didn't have time to teach me fancy sewing anymore. Now she spent her time trying to grow more food. At night we sat together, knitting socks and rolling bandages.

There were no more dances or barbecues. There wasn't any social life at all.

There was just the war now. It hung over everything. People were either talking about the war or worrying about their menfolk in the war. They also spent a lot of time waiting for letters with news about the war.

But for Keely and me, there was something else. There was the time after supper when we stole away to the big oak.

As the sun set and the sky faded to pink, we began the nightly lessons. We started with the alphabet.

At first I printed the letters as I said them aloud. Then Keely traced over them. She repeated them with me. Next she wrote the letters herself and said them alone.

Keely learned quickly. I often felt guilty about time I had spent with my tutor. I had been lazy. I'd never worked as hard as I should have. I hadn't been interested in learning. It had never seemed that I'd have much use for it.

THE FREEDOM TREE

The first word Keely learned was her name. After I wrote down the letters, she traced them. Then I said, "That's your name."

She stared at the paper. "Truly?"

I smiled. "Truly."

Keely lifted the paper with both hands. She brought it close to her face. "My name," she whispered. She sounded as if she were at church.

She set the paper down. Her eyes were far away. She was looking past the fields, past the river, past the swamp and the woods. She was staring past the here and now.

"I wish I could tell my daddy what I can do," Keely whispered.

Her soft words tore at my heart.

Keely's father was Big Cal. Two years before, he'd been caught trying to escape. As his punishment, he'd been sold to a plantation in Mississippi.

HOME

I wrote the letters down and said the word. Then Keely did the same.

It was twilight now. Everything was quiet. Shadows were creeping over the hills and grass. I felt as if Keely and I were wrapped in stillness. We were locked in our own special world.

I looked down at Keely's bent head. Learning meant so much to her. Without thinking, I wrote down another word and said it out loud.

FATHER

Keely looked at me quickly. Then she looked away. Her fingers grasped the pencil tightly. I thought it would break. With hard strokes, she traced over the word. When she said it aloud, her voice was shaking.

I hadn't been able to bear seeing Keely for three days after her father was sold. I had been filled with too much sadness. I'd felt bad for her and for Ellie. And I'd been strangely angry at Big Cal. I was mad that he had tried to run away. He had caused so much unhappiness for his family.

"Why did Big Cal do it?" I'd asked Ellie.

Ellie's eyes had been red-rimmed from crying. Slowly she'd moved around my mother's room, cleaning and straightening.

"It was something he had to do," Ellie had answered.

"I don't understand."

"No, child," Ellie had said. "I expect you wouldn't. But, you see, freedom was always mighty important to Cal. It was his dream. He had to try to make it come true. I can't be angry at him for that."

THE FREEDOM TREE

"But wasn't he happy here? He seemed happy," I'd said.

Ellie had smiled at me. But her smile had been sad. "Seeming and being are two different things, young miss."

Seeming and being—I thought about Ellie's words now. How many slaves were seeming to be one thing on the outside while being something else on the inside? Were all slaves living one life while wanting another?

Keely hadn't seemed to mind not being able to read or write. But inside, she'd wanted it terribly. Seeming and being—was that the life of a slave?

Lots of folks said the South was fighting the war so we could keep our slaves. Father disagreed.

"We're fighting to defend a state's right to leave the Union if it wants to," he'd always said. "If the North would leave us alone, we'd get rid of slavery ourselves. It would only take a generation or two."

A generation or two, I thought now. That meant that if Keely married and had children, those children would be slaves too. I wondered if Keely wanted to wait that long for freedom.

"Caroline!"

Mother's sharp voice cut across my thoughts. I got to my feet quickly.

"Caroline! Come quickly!"

An icy hand seemed to close around my heart. Mother never called me by my full name unless she was angry—or frightened.

I started running down the hill.

3
The Prisoner

Mother sat in the rocking chair on the porch. She was completely still. Her hands were tightly closed over a crumpled sheet of paper.

Ellie stood behind my mother. One of her hands rested on Mother's shoulder. Ellie pointed to the paper in my mother's hands. I took it from her. It was a letter from Tad.

Dear Mother and Caro,
I have sad news to tell you.

The cold hand of fear squeezed my heart tightly. I felt as if I couldn't breathe. I forced myself to keep reading.

Two days ago, Father went on a scouting mission. His group was attacked by Yankees. The rest of the scouting party reported that Father volunteered to hold off the enemy so they could escape. We have received word that Father has been taken prisoner.
I am so proud of him! He put his friends' lives before his own. Our colonel said that Father will receive a medal for bravery.

I pressed my lips together, trying to keep from crying. But the tears came anyway. Slowly they seeped from the corners of my eyes. It was so like Father to take a stand instead of riding away. I could see it all so clearly. My proud father almost daring the Yankees to take him.

THE FREEDOM TREE

Father has been taken to Rock Island Prison in Illinois. I will be honest. Conditions there are more terrible than I can say. Sickness is everywhere. The prisoners are barely fed. Although as a soldier in the Southern army, Father will be used to that.

But we must take heart. Father is a strong man. If anyone can survive in that dreadful place, he can.

I am well. Hope you are the same. I send my love to you both. I will write again when I can.

Your devoted son and brother,
Tad

I sank down on the porch. I tried to make myself understand the words I'd just read.

My father had been captured by the Yankees. Lawrence Haverton, one of the richest men in Georgia, was a prisoner. He was most certainly starving and maybe sick. It was unbelievable. And yet . . . it was true.

I looked down quickly at Tad's letter. It was dated more than two months ago. By now, Father could be—

No! I wouldn't let myself think that way. I

The Prisoner

would take heart as Tad had written. And I would help my mother do the same.

I knelt down in front of her. Carefully I folded the letter and placed it in her lap. Her hands closed around it.

"Did you hear, Mother?" I asked her. "Father will get a medal."

She didn't answer. I continued on, saying all the things I knew I should.

"You know how stubborn Father can be when he sets his mind to something. He won't let the Yankees get the best of him."

Mother shook her head slowly from side to side. "This war could go on for years—forever! How long can even a strong man last shut up in a place like that?"

Mother buried her head in her hands. Loud sobs shook her body. Her tears fell over the letter. I sat back on my heels. I was unsure what to do.

I'd never seen Mother like this. She'd never even shed a tear on the day Father and Tad had ridden off to war.

Instead, she'd stood proudly on the porch. Her bright blond hair had been piled high on her head. Her blue eyes had glittered as grandly as the string of beads around her neck. She'd been wearing a beautiful gown of satin and lace.

"I dressed special for this day, Caro," she'd told me as we waved good-bye. "As if I were going to a party. It's how I want my husband to remember me."

How beautiful Mother had looked that day. I'd always wanted to look like her. She was as fair-haired and rosy-lipped as a doll.

But I take after Father. My hair is as black as my mother's is blond. Ellie always says my brown eyes were put in with a sooty finger because my lashes and brows are so dark.

My mother and I had stood together on the porch long after the men had gone. She'd put her arm around my shoulders.

"We must stay cheerful until our men return," she'd said. "It's our duty as Southern ladies. It won't be for long. Our gentlemen will be victorious over that Yankee riffraff in a week or two. A month at the most!"

Now, Mother's sobs turned into a soft sound. She almost sounded like a kitten mewing for dinner.

"It gets so cold in Illinois in the winter," she moaned. "It snows all the time. Your father is unused to such weather, Caro. Whatever will he do?"

Mother shook her head again slowly. Ellie put a

hand beneath Mother's elbow. Gently Ellie lifted my mother to her feet.

"I'm going to take you upstairs, Miss Leandra. You need to lie down. I'll bring you a cool cloth for your forehead."

The two women, one black, one white, went inside. In the growing darkness, Keely and I sat together on the porch.

Keely! With a start, I realized that my father was now as powerless as Big Cal. Now it was the Yankees who would decide where and how Lawrence Haverton lived. They would choose when he would sleep and what he would eat. If he disobeyed, they could punish him—or worse.

Slaves had no say in their lives. They had no rights. And now, neither did my father.

I remembered the day I'd heard that my father was going to sell Keely's father. Mother had asked him not to. But he'd refused to listen to her.

"I'm good to my slaves," he'd said. "You know that. I feed them well. I never use the whip. But Cal has disobeyed. He must be punished. We must set an example for the others."

Mother had said nothing more. As much as she loved Ellie, she wouldn't go against her husband.

"Your father is right," she'd said to me. "Slaves must be taught their place."

THE FREEDOM TREE

I'd never thought of speaking up for Big Cal myself. I'd just accepted his being sold like I'd accepted all the other rules in my life. Yet now I was starting to understand how it must be for Keely and her family.

I burned with shame. I'd let my best friend's father be taken from her. I'd never even said a word.

Big Cal had been sent to Mississippi, never to return. Keely had lost a father. Ellie had lost a husband. He had been sold as if he were no more than a bale of cotton or a pack of pins.

Because in truth, that's what he was considered—a thing. Big Cal had belonged to my father. My father could do whatever he pleased with him.

It was the same with Ellie. She belonged to my mother.

Ellie had looked after me since birth. Her sweet voice had soothed me when I cried. Her gentle hands had picked me up when I fell. She was as dear to me as my mother.

But as much as I loved Ellie—as much as my mother loved her—she was still our slave. And so was Keely.

Keely had grown up in a slave cabin. I'd grown up in the "big house," as the slaves called it. Of course I'd been aware of the great differences in our lives. But I'd never really thought about it. That was just the way things were.

I'd lived with slavery my whole life, just like Mother and Father. But I'd never thought about what it meant.

But now I wondered. What would it be like to be a slave? What would it feel like to belong to someone else? How would it feel to know that at any minute, you could be sold or whipped or even killed if your owner had a mind to?

How would Father endure it? And how was I going to make it through the days, the months, maybe the years, of knowing that he was imprisoned?

"Keely," I said slowly, "how did you go on when your father was sold?"

I heard Keely draw in a breath in surprise. She was silent for a moment. Then she hugged her knees to her chest and spoke softly.

"At first, I tried not to think about it. Mama told me that was the best way. But I couldn't. I couldn't *not* think about it. It hurt so bad. And the hurt went so deep."

Keely paused. The night was warm. The rich smell of flowers hung thickly in the quiet air. Softly she went on.

"Then I found this place inside me, Miss Caro. Deep inside my soul. When I get to missing Daddy so much my heart hurts, I go there. And when I get to feeling sad about things too. In that place, I'm strong. No one and nothing can touch me there."

Keely's voice deepened. "As long as I'm strong in my soul, I have hope."

"I should have helped your father, Keely," I blurted out. It was hard to say the words. It was harder still to admit how I'd let her down.

"I should have said or done something," I admitted shamefully.

"Don't go worrying about it, Miss Caro." Keely's voice had the ring of someone who'd faced the truth. "There wasn't anything you could have done."

There was nothing to do now either. All I could do was wait. And I could pray that someday I would see my father again.

4
Gone Forever

In July 1863, the South lost the biggest battle of the war. It was fought in Gettysburg, Pennsylvania.

THE FREEDOM TREE

Mrs. Calvin, our neighbor, told us about it. She'd heard about it from a relative in Atlanta. Mail was even slower now. So news had to be passed from person to person.

The South lost again at Vicksburg, Mississippi. Then almost the whole state of Tennessee was captured by the Yankees.

Tad came home on leave that Christmas. He was in high spirits the whole week he spent at The Cedars. Or at least he tried to be. He tried hard to be the same carefree boy he'd been when he'd ridden off.

But there was a difference. He looked older. There were lines around his eyes and mouth. He had grown a mustache while he was away. He was thinner too. His once beautiful uniform was faded and patched.

But it was more than that. It was something beneath the surface. There was something grim that he was trying to hide.

He told us jokes about army life. He told us stories about his fellow soldiers. He promised that the South would win the war. He even told us that Father would be fine.

But the whole time, I knew he was telling us lies. And I knew why. He couldn't bring himself to tell us the truth.

The truth at The Cedars was that day by day, Mother was slipping away. Physically she was fine. But her mind was not the same. She seemed to live in some half-world of memories. She couldn't seem to face what was happening.

Mother and I said good-bye to Tad on the porch. In the cold light of a gray morning, Mother clung to her son as if she'd never let go. Very gently, he moved away from her. Then he bent down to give me a quick hug.

"Promise me you'll take care of Mother," he whispered. "She doesn't seem well."

With a smile that was too bright, Tad ran down the stairs. He jumped into the saddle. With a quick wave of his hand, he rode off. He rode down the long avenue and back to the war.

January and February of 1864 were colder than usual. I lined Mother's and my old dresses with cut-up carpet to keep out the wind. No one could afford new dresses now. We couldn't afford *anything*.

With the South completely blocked in, we couldn't sell our cotton. As a result, we had no money. No one in the South seemed to have money now. And even if we had, there was nothing to buy.

THE FREEDOM TREE

Before the war, there had been only a handful of factories in the South. Most of those had been destroyed by the Yankees. The ones that were left were turning out supplies for the war. That meant the rest of us had to make do with what we had.

Our dresses were patched and patched again. If I lost a button, there was none to replace it. I wrapped old cloth around an acorn and used that instead.

If our shoes got a hole, we lined them with cardboard. In the summer, I went barefoot to save leather.

All the little things I had once taken for granted were gone. Cut thorns were our sewing needles. We made our own soap and even our own ink. In fact, ink was so scarce, the newspaper in Atlanta had shut down.

Writing paper was scarce too. I taught Keely on pieces of old wallpaper and brown wrapping paper.

When we did get a letter from Tad, we crossed out his words and wrote above them. Then we mailed the same letter back.

But I never complained. I couldn't. For as hard as things were on us, they were much worse for our soldiers.

The hospitals were desperate for medicine. Very little could be slipped in through enemy lines. Bandages were never thrown out. They were washed and used again—and rewashed and reused.

When a soldier's uniform wore out, there was no gray cloth to replace it. Instead he had to wear homespun, loosely woven cloth. Usually it was dyed a butternut color.

Sometimes the soldiers would take a uniform off a dead Yankee and wear it. Our men took the boots and guns off dead and captured Yankees too.

Food was also in short supply all over the South. Once, I ate waffles dripping with butter for breakfast. I had ham and golden biscuits for lunch. Long ago, every dinner had been a feast. And every feast had been topped off with chocolate layer cake or strawberry shortcake.

Now the table at The Cedars was set with yams and apples, yams and peaches, yams and peanuts, or yams and milk. I was beginning to hate yams!

The commissary troop took almost all our livestock. We had no chickens left. We had only one cow, one horse, a sow, and her litter of piglets.

Every day I looked greedily at those pigs. But I knew Ellie wanted them to get bigger before she slaughtered them. They were so small now. They wouldn't make much of a meal.

I understood that. But I was also afraid the commissary troop would take the pigs before we could eat them.

THE FREEDOM TREE

Ellie made tea out of dried leaves and coffee out of boiled corn. She used honey or molasses instead of sugar. When she cooked up the tough old rooster, we thought it was a treat!

Ellie was cooking because almost all of our slaves were gone. Most of the men had been taken by the Southern army. They were needed to dig rifle pits and trenches. Most of the women and men who were left had run off to find the Yankee lines—and freedom.

Ellie, Keely, Betsy, May, Jack, and Ben were the six slaves left. Once there had been over a hundred slaves living in the slave cabins.

Once, the hardest work I did was lift a fan. Now I worked right beside Keely in the kitchen, the garden, and the orchard. Now I wished I knew less French and more about cooking and canning peaches.

In days past, Ellie had bleached away my freckles. Milk-white skin was highly prized by Southern ladies. Now my arms and neck were dotted with freckles. I wore a sunbonnet when I worked outside. But even my face was sprouting freckles now.

Long ago, my mother had been a proud woman. She'd loved to say that just one more victory would send those Yankees running. These days, my mother drifted around the house like a sleepwalker.

Now Ellie and I were trying to run The Cedars. Every morning, Ellie settled Mother on the porch. She put a basket of mending on her lap. Sometimes Mother would sew for hours. Other times, the needle would fall from her hands and she'd simply sit there in silence.

I had promised Tad that I'd look after Mother. So I was trying to be patient with her. I wished I could be as patient as Ellie was. I tried to speak kindly to Mother. But it was hard.

Sometimes Mother would get up from the porch and run anxiously from room to room. When we asked her what she was doing, she said she was looking for something. But she could never tell us what. I thought maybe she was trying to find her old life.

Sometimes I wanted to run in search of my old life too. I wanted to run to my mother for comfort. I wanted to tell her how scared and tired I was. I wanted her to make things all right again like she had done when I was small.

But that woman was gone forever. And so was the life she led.

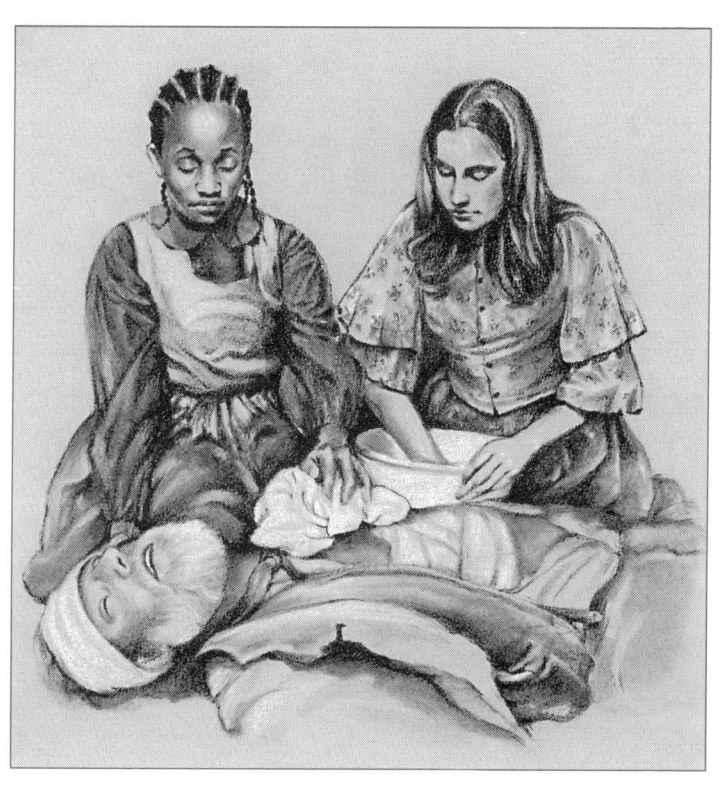

5
Yankees

Spring gave way to a warm summer. Yankee troops were on the move all over Georgia. For the first time, we could hear the sounds of battle at The Cedars.

At first I thought the low rumble was thunder. Then I realized it was cannon fire. I tried not to hear it. I tried to push the sound away. And I tried not to let myself wonder if the rumble was growing closer.

Our Southern troops were on the march too. Quite often they passed by The Cedars. I'd run down to the road to cheer them on. I carried a bucket of drinking water and a dipper in my hands.

The soldiers always thanked me for my kindness. I couldn't help noticing how tired they looked. No, they were more than tired. They were bone-weary.

Their faces were streaked with dirt, dust, and gunpowder. Their uniforms were ragged. Some of them had an arm in a sling. Others wore bandages around their heads. Still others stumped by on one good leg and one wooden peg.

The South needed every man it had. Even wounded and half-whole men were needed. Boys as young as 13 and 14 were joining the army now. They marched beside old men with gray whiskers.

❧ ❧ ❧ ❧ ❧

August dawned hotter than July. Every day, wagons full of injured soldiers passed down the long avenue of cedar trees and up to our front door. The wounded soldiers were carried into the house.

THE FREEDOM TREE

They were placed on sofas, beds, chairs, and even tables. When all those were filled, the soldiers were put on the floor.

Keely and I tore towels, sheets, pillowcases, curtains, and petticoats into bandages. Then we'd stand by Ellie or Betsy or May as they pried bullets out of moaning men's bodies. The basins we held slowly filled with blood.

Sometimes as I stood there, my head would swim. The smell of unwashed injured flesh rose around me. The heat was dizzying.

But as soon as I opened a window, gnats, mosquitoes, and swarms of flies shot in. Then I'd have to fan the men to keep the bugs away from their wounds. I'd wave my fan until my arms ached. I thought of all the hours Keely had fanned me.

The worst times were when I had to pick maggots and lice out of the wounds. Then I almost gagged. But I didn't. I didn't faint either. I wouldn't let myself.

Even when the hot days became hot nights, I didn't give in. I'd clench my teeth and shut my eyes. I'd say to myself, "If these men can do the fighting, you can do the nursing."

I promised myself that I'd hang on a little longer. I'd hang on like so many of our men were doing. I wouldn't give up—just like all of the South wasn't giving up.

Harder even than the nursing were the burials. Jack and Ben would dig a grave in the Haverton burial ground. Everyone would gather round. I'd mark a passage for Mother to read out of the Bible. It often seemed she hardly knew what she was saying.

We'd all say a short prayer. Then the soldier's body, wrapped in a sheet, would be lowered into the ground. Sometimes we didn't even know the man's name.

I couldn't keep the tears away at these quick funerals. I always wondered if somewhere, on some unknown plantation, Tad's body was being lowered into a grave.

As more and more of our troops marched by, the sound of battle was always in our ears. Now we could hear the cracking of rifles as well as cannons. More and more wounded men flooded The Cedars. They were carried in farm wagons, ox carts, and even carriages.

One day blurred into the next. I ordered myself to carry on.

Give water to the soldiers on the march. Give water to the injured. Pass out what food we had. Keep away the flies. Cheer the wounded as best you can. Bury the dead.

THE FREEDOM TREE

Don't notice that your arms ache. Ignore that your dress is streaked with dirt and blood and sweat. Push away the dark thoughts. Whenever there's time, steal away to the big oak for a lesson.

Keely was reading now. I sneaked books out of Father's library for her. She read *Ivanhoe* and *Treasure Island*. When she had trouble with words, I'd help her sound them out.

One day I handed her Father's favorite book, *The Three Musketeers*. As she read, I stretched out on the ground. The shade from the tree's thick branches fell welcome and cool over my face. It was midday, and the sun was at its full height.

For several days now, there had been no wounded. Nor had any of our soldiers marched by The Cedars. The sounds of battle had stopped. In a strange way, the quiet was even more frightening than the noise.

Why were the guns silent? What did it mean? Where were our men? Most frightening of all, where were the Yankees?

I turned over on my side as Keely read on. I sighed. I was always grateful for these peaceful moments.

The crack of a bullwhip cut the air.

I scrambled to my feet. So did Keely. We stared at my mother. Her face was furious.

"I knew it!" Mother screamed. "I knew you were teaching Keely! I've watched you two sneaking up here with paper and pencil. I saw you steal books from your father's library."

Mother gave the whip another crack. I jumped. I could feel Keely trembling.

My ladylike mother had completely disappeared. In her place was a wild woman with tumbled hair. Anger raged in every line of her body.

"I'll punish *you* later," Mother snapped at me. She took a step toward Keely. "But I'm going to whip the hide right off *you*, girl! You have disobeyed. You have broken the rules."

Quickly I stepped in front of Keely. "You can't do this, Mother! The old laws—the old ways—they don't matter anymore. Everything is different now."

Mother's eyes blazed. "What are you talking about? You should know better than anyone what's proper. You are Miss Caroline Haverton."

Her voice rose to a wild note. "You are from one of the finest families in the South!"

Mother's way of life had crumbled about her. Now, as I watched, she was crumbling under the weight of war and worry and fear. But still I had to try to reason with her.

"Father never hurt any of our slaves," I said. "He wouldn't like it if you did." I reached out a hand to Mother. "Give me the whip."

Mother slapped my hand away. She flicked the lash meaningfully at Keely.

THE FREEDOM TREE

"I will do what I must," she declared. "And no one will stop me!"

Mother fixed Keely with blue eyes as hard as stone. "Come here, girl," she hissed. "Face your punishment!"

"No!" I flung out both arms wide. "You can't hurt Keely. I won't let you. She deserves to be educated!"

"You're talking nonsense," Mother said. "Keely is a slave. She deserves only what we give her."

Mother grabbed Keely by the arm. I heard Keely moan. Mother flung the girl to the ground. She raised the whip over her head. I stared at the braided rawhide and the nail head at the end of the lash. I thought of how it would tear at Keely's flesh.

The whip was curling through the air. Before it could land, I pushed Keely out of the way. The lash fell on my arm. I cried out in pain.

Keely screamed. Mother dropped the whip.

"Why did you do that, Caro?" she cried.

I put my hand on my arm. My white skin was gashed with blood.

Keely rushed to my side. "You have to let Mama look at your arm, Miss Caro. She can soothe it."

But I couldn't seem to move. I just stood there, watching the blood seep between my fingers. I listened to my mother cry.

Keely pleaded with me, "Come on, Miss Caro."

I took one stumbling step and then another.

Suddenly we heard the pounding of hooves. We heard someone yelling.

Mrs. Calvin was riding down our drive as if an army of demons were chasing her. She didn't slow down as she galloped toward the porch. She just pointed behind her.

"Yankees!" Mrs. Calvin yelled. "The Yankees are marching down the road!"

6
No Time to Lose

Mother stared at me. Her fury of a moment ago had passed.

"I don't understand," she said. "What's happening? Is someone coming?"

I took Mother by the shoulders. "You must go back to the house," I said gently but firmly. "You must go now!"

"Go back to the house," Mother repeated. She started off like a child.

My heart was pounding. But I wasn't afraid. I was thinking too quickly to feel fear. My brain was as cold and clear as ice water.

We'd already hidden the silverware and Mother's jewelry in the narrow space under the porch. But we had other things the Yankees would want.

I turned to Keely. "Tell Ben and Jack to hide the cow and horse. Tell your mother and Betsy to take all the food out of the kitchen and bury it in the woods. Then you and May take the piglets and head for the swamp."

Keely didn't answer. She just took off like a shot.

I ran across the pasture to the sow's pen. I picked up a stick and started driving the sow toward the swamp. The animal snorted angrily as I swung my stick. I gritted my teeth and forced her forward. There was no time to lose!

I could hear the piglets squealing. In the distance, the cow was bawling. I hoped the Yankees couldn't hear them.

THE FREEDOM TREE

No time to lose, I thought again and again. I was panting so hard, I thought my corset would burst.

This was my last day in a corset, I promised myself. Corsets might be fine for ladies, but I wasn't sure I was a lady anymore.

We turned the pigs loose in the swamp. Wiping my streaming forehead, I thanked May and Keely.

"This is the last thing I'm going to do for your family," May said. "Betsy too. And Jack and Ben."

"Wh—what do you mean?"

"I mean we're going with the Yankees," May answered. "We're going north to live free. We've already decided."

She looked down for a moment as if feeling ashamed. But just for a moment. Then she lifted her head again.

"I'm sorry to leave you all alone, Miss Caro. But it's what we have to do."

I forced a small smile. "Have a safe journey, May."

"Thank you, miss," May said.

She started off as quick as a rabbit. Then suddenly, she skidded to a stop. She looked fearfully over one shoulder.

"You don't think the Yankees will hurt us, do

you, Miss Caro?"

I paused. I could lie and say, "Yes, the Yankees will hurt you! They'll beat you and starve you!" If I did, maybe May would tell the others, and they wouldn't go.

But I couldn't. What I'd told my mother was true. Everything was different now. May, Betsy, Jack, and Ben deserved their chance for a new life in this new world.

"The Yankees won't harm you," I said. I made a little shooing motion with both hands. "Get along now. It'll be all right."

May took off. I couldn't look at Keely. I couldn't ask her the question I knew I should. I couldn't ask it because I was too afraid of the answer.

Would Keely and Ellie leave too?

"We'd best get back to the house, Miss Caro," Keely said. I nodded. Now wasn't the time to stand around worrying. I had to get back to Mother. She couldn't be left to face the enemy alone.

We slogged through the swamp. We ran across the fields and back to the house. All the while I was wondering where the Yankees were. Had they come yet? And when they did come, what would they do?

THE FREEDOM TREE

We'd all heard how terrible the Yankees were. We'd heard the stories about how the Yankees had robbed and looted. We'd heard about how they'd burned down houses with the people still inside. Many people believed the Yankees wanted to destroy every man, woman, and child in the South.

I was never sure I believed all the rumors, but who could say? Maybe they were true. And if they were, then those evil monsters were heading for my house.

I dashed inside. Keely was at my heels.

Quickly I cried out, "Mother! Mother, where are you?"

"Here I am, Caro," Mother answered. She stepped out of the parlor. "What are you shouting about, daughter? Haven't I told you that a lady doesn't raise her voice?"

Mother brushed a hand across her face as if chasing away a cobweb. "I wonder what's keeping your father," she said dreamily. "He's late for lunch. That isn't like him."

"My fa—" I was ready to remind her of just exactly where Lawrence Haverton was. Then my lips clamped together. My heart turned over.

Between those terrible moments at the big oak and now, Mother had completely lost the years just gone by. She'd returned in her mind to happier days when the world made sense.

I could hear the sound of hooves pounding down the avenue. Any minute now, blue-coated soldiers would sweep into The Cedars.

Mother glanced out one of the long windows. "Do we have company?"

Indeed we do, I thought grimly. But Mother couldn't deal with the Yankees now. She probably never could. Just seeing soldiers in her house could force her over the edge. To what, I didn't want to think about.

But what to do with her? I wondered wildly.

"My mama said for me to bring you to the woods, Miss Leandra," Keely said smoothly. "She's set up a picnic. We must be going. We don't want to keep Mama waiting."

I pressed Keely's hand. "Thank you, Keely," I breathed. "Thank you for taking Mother to the . . . picnic."

Quickly, Keely led Mother down the hall to the back door.

I straightened my hair as best I could. I ran to the barrel of drinking water that stood in the kitchen. I washed the mud from my face and hands. I cleaned the blood from my stinging arm. With a sharp movement, I flung off my apron.

THE FREEDOM TREE

I took a deep breath. Then I headed out the door and down the steps to meet the Yankees.

7
Not Alone

A double row of soldiers rode up to the house. The lieutenant called for them to dismount. Some of the men were ordered into the fields. Others were directed into the house.

THE FREEDOM TREE

As the soldiers swarmed by me, I tried to keep my head up. I kept my back straight. I wasn't afraid, but I was burning with anger.

I wasn't angry at just the Yankees. I was angry at everyone who had started this war and then left women and children to finish it.

The lieutenant folded his arms and leaned against a post. His forage cap was low on his head. Under the visor, his little eyes gleamed.

"General Sherman's marching through Georgia, miss," he said. "From Atlanta to the sea, the Union army's taking this state. We've got orders to seize all the food and livestock we can find. The general told us to pick Georgia clean."

"You can't tell me all those men in the house are just looking for food," I said coldly.

"Some of my men do like to pick up a few valuables, miss," the lieutenant said. Then he smiled nastily. He scratched his head.

"I try to stop them, miss. But what can I do?" He spread his hands wide. "I'm just one man."

And what could I do? I thought. I was one young girl against the might of Sherman's army. All I could do was listen to the enemy as they tramped through the house. All I could do was shut my eyes to the sound of crashing china and shattering glass.

Not Alone

The Yankees weren't evil. They were just ordinary men who had their orders. They were men who wanted to get back a little of what the war had cost them. And smashing Southern homes and stealing Southern goods was how they were doing it.

A tall sergeant with a drooping mustache came out of the house. He ran down the steps. In his hands was an ashtray. It was my father's ashtray. My heart ached. I remembered all the times I'd seen Father's cigar rest in that ashtray.

A bowlegged soldier in a dirty coat shoved his way out the door. A young soldier was behind him. The bowlegged man glanced at me angrily.

"I reckon this little lady here has hidden all the most valuable things. We couldn't find any jewelry."

The young soldier looked pointedly at the silver picture frame in the other man's hands. "You've done all right," he said.

The bowlegged man laughed. He clapped the young soldier on the back. "I sure have, sonny!" He clattered down the stairs.

The young soldier looked at me. He seemed almost ashamed. "I'm sorry for your inconvenience, miss."

I said nothing. I only nodded my head.

"You don't have to apologize," the lieutenant said sternly.

The young soldier turned red. "Maybe I do, sir. I have three sisters at home. I'd hate to leave them in the fix we're leaving folks here."

The young soldier tipped his cap and went down the stairs.

Singly and in groups, the other soldiers tramped out of the house. Most of them carried some small treasure. A few carried larger items.

I watched as pieces of china, a candlestick, my mother's silver-backed brush, blankets, goblets, and clothes were carried away. One man even carried a chair. Another hauled a footstool down the steps.

One of the soldiers who had been sent out to the fields came into view. He was leading the horse. My heart sank. It was our last horse. Now it belonged to the Yankees.

"Is that all you found?" the lieutenant called out.

"Sure is," the soldier called back. "These folks don't have much."

The lieutenant grinned. "They have even less now."

The rest of the soldiers were coming in from the fields. One of them reported that they'd set fire to all the outbuildings. The slave cabins, the barn, the stable, and the smokehouse were burning.

The lieutenant nodded his approval. He turned to me and raised his cap in a mock salute.

"Well, little lady," he said, "we've given you something to remember us by."

The lieutenant ran down the stairs and mounted up. He held up a hand to his men and called out a command. The line of soldiers rode off down the avenue, spurs jingling. Most of the saddles were laden with stolen goods. Betsy, May, Jack, and Ben rode behind four of the soldiers.

My head dropped. Now that the Yankees couldn't see me, the tears started. I walked through the house slowly.

Mirrors were broken. Pictures were ripped out of their frames. Glass littered the floor. All of Mother's framed needlework had been torn up. Chairs and tables had been smashed. The once-gleaming wooden floor was scarred and pitted.

I went upstairs. Every mattress and pillow had been ripped apart. The air was thick with feathers. Every drawer in every dresser had been pulled out and dumped upside down.

Yankee hands had gone through all of our belongings. Hated enemy hands had pawed through everything I loved and treasured.

I remembered Christmases and birthdays. I thought about lazy summer mornings and cozy winter nights. But now every memory had been touched by the Yankees.

I felt as if my own body had been attacked. I was still crying. I cried for The Cedars, for my father, and for my brother. I wept for all the men so far from home—and for all the men who would never return home.

I felt almost too weary to stand. I leaned one arm against a wall. I didn't even have the strength to wipe the tears away. I thought about all the struggle and loss. What had it all been for?

Suddenly I smelled smoke. My head jerked up. My body straightened. Then I was running down the stairs.

A spark from one of the outbuildings must have jumped to the kitchen. Smoke was spilling out the door. Flames were creeping across the floor.

I had to put out the fire before it leaped from the kitchen into the hall. I had to stop it before it raged through the house.

I ran into the parlor and grabbed a rug. I dipped it into the barrel of drinking water.

Coughing and choking, I tried to smother the flames. I swung my rug up and down. Again and again, I beat at the fire.

I'll never do it, I thought. I'll never do it alone. The Cedars is lost!

And then I wasn't alone. Suddenly Keely was beside me. She held a wet rug in her hands too. Together we worked away.

Near-blind from the smoke, we slapped at the fire. We swung our rugs up and down, back and forth.

Finally we put the fire out. Our faces were scorched and sooty. Our skin was smarting. Our throats were burning. But the fire was out.

Keely and I staggered out to the porch. We sagged down on the steps. Gratefully we breathed in the fresh air.

Thick clouds of smoke curled up from the outbuildings. The air was thick with the smell of it. But the house was safe. My home was safe.

I gasped out my thanks to Keely. But there was something else I had to say. I couldn't put it off any longer.

"The others rode off with the Yankees," I began.

We were both still struggling for breath. It was a moment before I could continue.

"Don't you want to go too?" I asked. "It's not too late."

"I thought about it," Keely admitted. "But I owe

you a powerful lot, Miss Caro. I won't forget that."

"You mean the reading and writing?" I shook my head. "That's no more than you deserved—"

Keely interrupted me. "I mean you were going to take a whipping for me. A body doesn't forget that. I won't leave you now. Not when you need me the most."

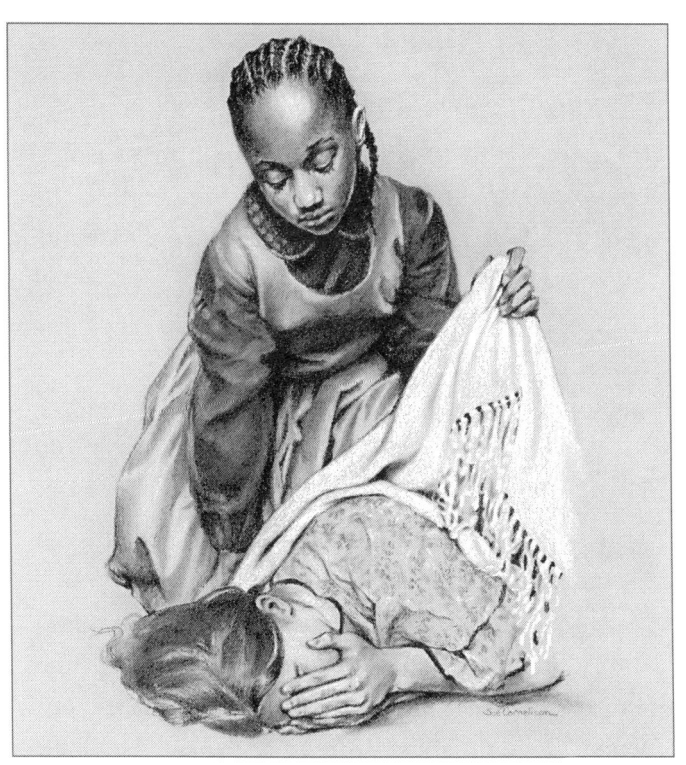

8
Strong in My Soul

We were completely cut off at The Cedars. Mrs. Calvin's plantation was only five miles away. But without a horse, it might as well have been across the country. I didn't have the time or energy to walk those miles.

THE FREEDOM TREE

Ellie had hidden our seeds from the Yankees. So there was a garden to plant. Soon there would be weeds to pull. There was firewood to be chopped. Water needed to be hauled from the well. The cow had to be milked.

Keely showed me how to set rabbit traps and fish lines in the river. We checked them twice a day.

We had dishes to wash and rooms to clean. There were always clothes to be mended.

I was busy all the time. I had a fine crop of blisters on both hands to show for it.

Every morning, for just a few seconds, I could almost imagine that I was still the old Caroline Haverton. That I was still the daughter of a rich planter. That my most difficult decision was which dress to wear.

I'd lie in bed, drifting between sleep and waking. Outside my window, the mockingbirds were singing. The sun would fall across my face. I could almost imagine I smelled bacon sizzling. I'd push up and stretch my arms over my head. And then I'd remember everything.

So I'd force myself to get up. I'd splash some water on my face. Then I'd pull on an old faded dress. Finally I'd start down the stairs to begin another day of grinding work.

One day Mrs. Calvin drove her wobbly wagon up to our plantation. She wanted to trade some of her chickens for two of our piglets. After we made the trade, Mrs. Calvin asked about Mother. With difficulty, I explained how things were.

Mrs. Calvin patted my hand. "My poor Caroline! I feel so sorry for you."

At that, I jerked my hand away. I stiffened my spine. I couldn't bear folks feeling sorry for me. It was hard enough not to feel sorry for myself.

Indian summer gave way to winter. Soon it was Christmas again. Ellie butchered a piglet. We ate fresh pork and stewed apples.

The lace tablecloth had been stolen. The table was scarred from Yankee bayonets. The plates were cracked and mismatched. There were no rugs on the floors. No pictures or paintings hung on the walls.

There was only one bewildered woman and one bitter young girl.

Mother suddenly called out to the kitchen. "Ellie, you must keep a plate warm for Mr. Haverton and Tad. They should be returning any time from Macon."

Mother smiled at me. "I hope you liked your presents, Caro. Father sent all the way to New York for them."

I jumped to my feet. Angrily, I ran from the table. I knocked down my chair.

Behind me, I could hear Mother's soft voice. "Whatever is wrong, Caroline?"

I ran out the door and down the steps. Almost unaware of where I was going, I headed up the hill to the big oak. I crumpled up on the ground, hugging my knees to my chest. There was a knot of pain at my center as hard and cold as ice.

I couldn't go on. I wouldn't go on. I'd just lie there under the bare branches. I would lie there until I became part of the ground and grass.

I wouldn't get up again until I couldn't feel anymore. I didn't want to feel any more sadness or loneliness. I didn't want to feel anything.

"I brought you a shawl, Miss Caro." Keely's voice came to me as if from far away.

"Go away. I don't want it."

Keely knelt beside me. "Maybe not," she said as she covered me with the shawl. "But you sure do need it. It's mighty cold out."

"I don't want it," I repeated. "I don't want anything."

Keely folded her arms and bent her head against the wind. She didn't pat me. She didn't make her voice all sugary. When she spoke, she sounded matter-of-fact.

"I know how you're feeling, Miss Caro. The day they took my daddy, I ran into the woods. I just lay there all curled up, just like you. I was going to go on lying there till it stopped hurting."

Her words pierced the icy sadness inside me. But I didn't move. I stayed curled up in misery. The chilly wind blew over us.

"Then I figured out that it wasn't ever going to stop," Keely continued. "The hurting, I mean. So I got up and started home. It was when I was walking back to the cabin that I found that place inside me. That secret place, where I can stand things. The hurt didn't go away. And I reckon yours won't either. But I got strong enough to stand it."

Keely unwrapped her arms. She reached out and took my hand.

"That's what you have to do, Miss Caro. You have to get strong in your soul. Once you do, there's nothing that can keep you down."

THE FREEDOM TREE

Very slowly, I pushed up to my knees. I gripped Keely's hand.

"I'll try, Keely," I said softly. "I'll try."

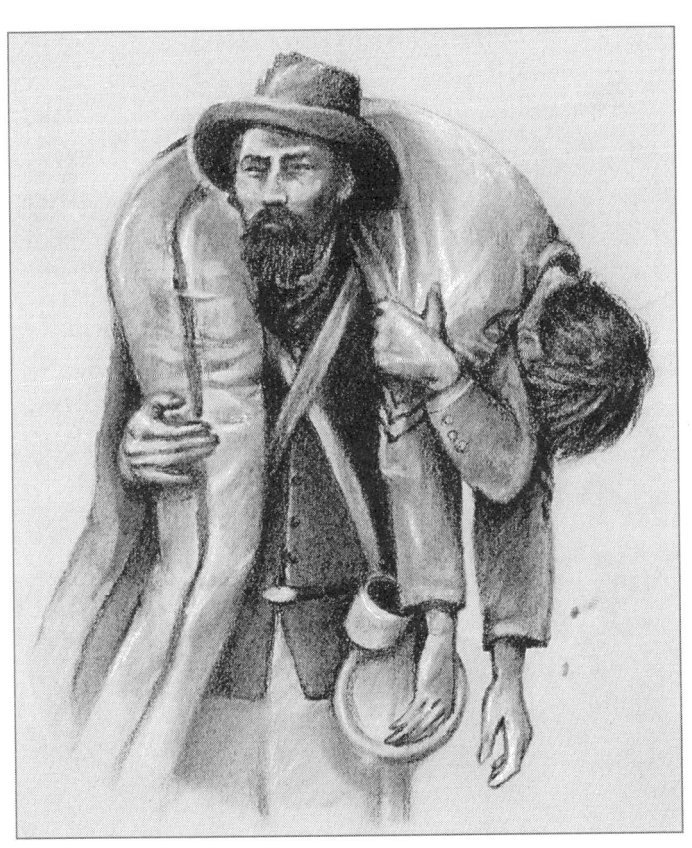

9
An End and a Beginning

That next April 1865, General Robert E. Lee surrendered to General Ulysses S. Grant. The war was over. The South had lost.

THE FREEDOM TREE

We didn't hear the news until several weeks later. Mrs. Calvin rode over to tell us.

It was hard to get used to the idea. It was all over. The war that had seemed to last longer than a lifetime was finally over.

Not that the end was a surprise. I'd seen it coming for a long time. I'd recognized it in the faces of the wounded soldiers in our parlor. I'd known from the blue-coated lieutenant's grin. I'd understood it in my mother's confused eyes.

The war was over. The South had lost. But somehow, the end was also a beginning.

Now I didn't mind the hard work. I knew that all the crops we grew and all the animals we raised would belong to us. The commissary troops couldn't take our food. The Yankees couldn't rob us.

The end of the war brought a steady stream of soldiers passing by The Cedars. They were ragged, bearded, and skinny. Most of them had no boots. Their feet were wrapped in rags. They looked more like scarecrows than men.

Most of them asked if they could sit a spell on our porch. Some requested a cool drink of water from our well. They all looked so weary from four years of fighting and starving. I wondered how many of them were going to make it home.

Of course, some of them had no homes to go to. Their farms and plantations had been destroyed. Their families had been scattered. Some had been killed.

Many of the returning soldiers were looking for a new life. They were just like me. We were all trying to find new hope.

When we could spare it, Keely and I gave the soldiers food. I asked every soldier if he knew Tad or Father. But none of them did. I began to wonder if my brother or father was ever coming home.

But one day, a tired horse with its ribs showing plodded up the avenue. An equally tired and skinny man was walking beside it. A body was draped across the horse's saddle. It was Tad.

At first sight, I feared the worst. But my brother wasn't dead. He was just very ill from sleeping too many nights in the rain.

The thin soldier lifted Tad from the saddle. He carried my brother into the house and up to his old room. He laid him carefully on the bed.

I tucked a ragged blanket up to Tad's chin. His skin was gray. His face was half-covered with a scraggly beard. His bones stuck out of his torn and dirty uniform.

But he was home. He was alive and he was home!

THE FREEDOM TREE

"My name's Lafe Peterson," the soldier said.

"Thank you for bringing my brother home," I said. The words seemed so little for such a big favor.

"Your brother was my lieutenant," Lafe answered. "He saved my skin more than once. Bringing him home was the least I could do.

"I'm going to leave the horse too," he continued. "Give him some rest and a little feed. Soon he'll look lively again." Lafe smiled. "So will your brother."

Lafe looked around the room. "The lieutenant talked a mighty lot about his home, miss. I feel like I know every inch of this place."

I smiled sadly. "The Cedars must look very different from the way Tad described it."

Lafe nodded. "And you too, miss. The lieutenant said you were a little girl. But you're not. You look about as strong and proud as a grown woman."

Lafe took off his cap and twisted it in his hands. He licked his lips.

"I—I have something to tell you, Miss Caroline. It's not easy to say, and it's not going to be easy to hear."

I sank down on the edge of the bed. With one hand, I gripped the post.

"It's about my father, isn't it?" I asked shakily. I tried to swallow over the huge lump in my throat.

"Tad came home," I whispered. "But my father

never will. That's what you're going to tell me, isn't it?"

Lafe looked down. "It is, Miss Caroline. We got word just after the surrender. Your father died in Rock Island about six months ago."

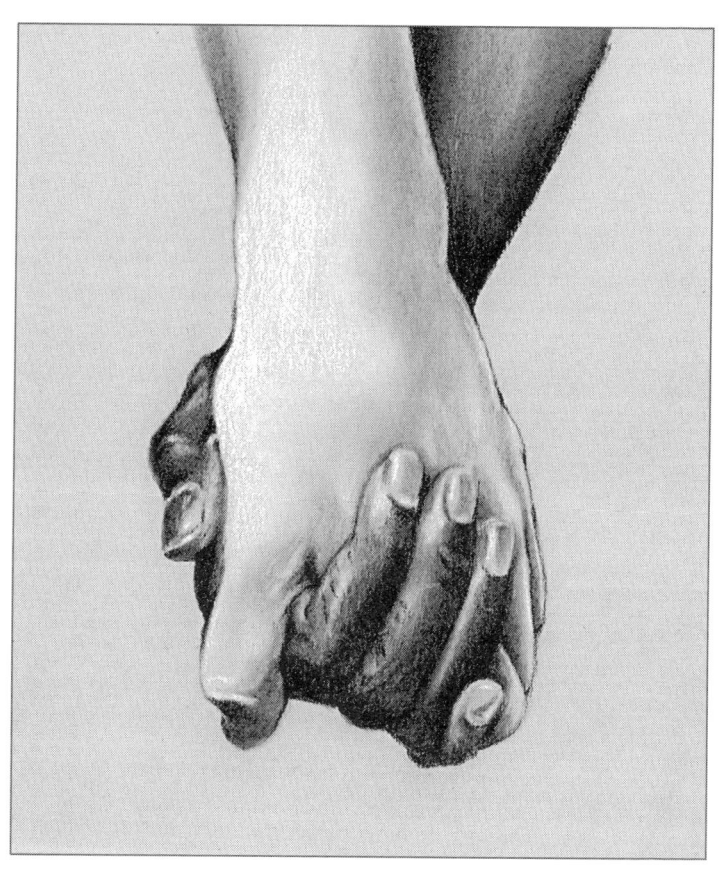

10
The Freedom Tree

Ellie and I told Mother about her husband. She didn't understand.

"I don't know what you're talking about," Mother said. "My husband is in Macon. He will return shortly."

Mother lifted up the skirts of her raggedy dress. She went out to the porch to begin another day.

"She'll go to her grave waiting for that man," Ellie said. "Maybe that's a blessing. If she woke up one morning and found things like they really are, she probably couldn't stand it."

Mother sometimes looked in on Tad. She thought he'd fallen in the hunting field. My brother was unconscious for days. Ellie sat with him during the day. Keely and I took turns at night.

Sometimes Tad would move restlessly against the sheets. His face would start to twitch. He'd call out to friends long since dead. He'd mumble about battles long since past.

I'd dampen a cloth and pass it over his feverish face. After a few minutes, he'd quiet down.

But one morning, Tad awoke to the world. For weeks afterward, he lay in bed. He stared quietly out the window.

I'd slip into his room whenever I could. We talked about Father. I explained about Mother.

We talked some about the war—but not much. Tad wanted to put the past behind him. So did I. It was the future I was interested in.

THE FREEDOM TREE

One evening I found Tad propped up against his pillow. It was the first time he'd been able to sit up. He smiled at me when I came into the room.

"Sometimes I thought I'd never see home again," he said.

I took Tad's hand. Together we looked out at the rolling fields and the setting sun.

"Father would be mighty happy the Yankees didn't take a torch to The Cedars," Tad said.

"They tried," I said shortly. "Keely and I put the fire out."

Tad looked at me in amazement. "Just you two?"

I laughed. "There wasn't anybody else."

"It's a real fine thing, Caro, the way you've kept this place going. Father would be proud of you."

"I'm not so sure about that," I answered. "I think he'd be horrified to know what I was up to. He thought ladies were meant for the parlor, not the plow."

"He'd have to change with the times," Tad said. Then he added softly, "If he could."

Still holding my brother's hand, I sat down on the chair next to his bed.

"Tad," I said eagerly, "I have a plan for The Cedars. I haven't told anyone, but it's been growing in my mind ever since the war ended. I know some

The Freedom Tree

of the folks around here are selling off their land. But I want to keep every acre. I want to make The Cedars like it was!"

I started moving excitedly around the room. I was filled with energy and dreams.

"We have enough food stored to make it through the winter. In the spring, we can plant cotton. We have plenty of seed. We couldn't plant many acres, not right away. But when we sell our first crop, we can buy more seed and plant more cotton."

Tad cut off my excited words. "It won't work, Caro. We don't have enough people to work the fields."

"I've thought about that too. There are so many men coming back from the war with no home to go to. Why couldn't we hire some? At first we could only give them food and a place to sleep. But once we make enough money, we could pay them."

I walked to the window again. "I want to see those fields white with cotton again. I want animals in the pasture. I want this whole place alive and growing again."

I turned to face my brother. "I know it will be hard. But what hasn't been these last years?"

"I've never heard you talk like this before," Tad said. He was looking at me in a way he never had before. He was staring at me with admiration.

THE FREEDOM TREE

"I didn't think you cared about what crops we planted," Tad said. "I didn't think you even noticed if they grew or not."

"I wasn't given a chance to care," I replied. "I wasn't given the chance to like or dislike anything. Mother and Father decided everything for me. And I let them."

I leaned out the window and took a deep breath. I filled my lungs with the warm air. The mockingbirds were in full voice. The pines stood dark against the sky. I could almost smell their sharp scent.

In my mind, I saw the swampy yellow water at the edge of the woods. I pictured the rich red soil in the fields. I remembered how it felt in my hands.

"For the first time in my life, Tad, I'm deciding things for myself. What I want. Who I want to be. And I know I want to stay here and make The Cedars bloom again."

"You've changed, Caro," Tad said wonderingly. "When I left . . . well, to be honest, you were just a spoiled little girl."

I certainly was, I thought grimly. I'd been a spoiled child who hadn't lifted a finger to save her best friend's father. I'd been so unaware of the suffering of those around me.

I turned back to Tad. "What do you think of my idea?"

The Freedom Tree

"I think it's a good one, Miss Caroline Haverton," he said. He sounded like the teasing brother I remembered. He took my hand and pulled me to his side again.

"I want you to be an equal partner," Tad said. "You have to promise me you won't change back into an empty-headed belle again. We're in this together."

He smiled, but I knew he was serious.

"No danger of that happening," I said.

I left him to rest. I had carried out one part of my plan. But there was one more thing I had to do.

I ran down the stairs and found Ellie. Then I hurried out the door. As I had so many times before, I headed for the big oak.

The pinkish color was fading from the sky. The air was as still as only country air can be. It was twilight. I knew this time of day would remind me of Keely and our hours together for the rest of my life.

I leaned my back against the trunk of the tree. I stared straight up into the spreading branches.

Under this tree, I'd taught Keely—and ended up learning more than she had. I had discovered myself and the person I didn't want to be.

Under this tree, I'd stood up against my mother and all I'd been taught. I'd stood up for what I'd come to believe in.

Under this tree, I'd learned about the strong place

in my soul. I now knew where real freedom was. For the first time in my life, I was free. I was free to make my own decisions. And I was free to lead my own life. Now I was the person I wanted to be.

My decision to stay at The Cedars would mean backbreaking work. It might mean years and years of being poor. But I didn't care. It was the path I'd chosen. And walking my own path would mean I'd stay free.

Keely came up the hill. "Mama said you wanted me to meet you here." She smiled. "I thought my lessons were all done, Miss Caro."

"Not quite."

I motioned for Keely to sit down. I pulled out a torn corner of wallpaper and a pencil. I started printing.

FREEDOM

"I know that word, Miss Caro," Keely said softly.

"I think you've known it in your heart forever," I said. "But I want you to learn about it for real. There's a Freedman's Bureau in Atlanta. The people there are helping former slaves start over. They can help you trace your father."

Keely's face lit up. "That's a fine idea, Miss Caro!"

I swallowed. The next idea would be harder to get out.

"The Freedman's Bureau is also starting schools

for former slaves," I said. "If you go to Atlanta, you can get a real education. You can learn all the things you'll need to make a new life for yourself. You might even want to go up north, Keely. They say there are lots of opportunities up there."

"Mama wants me to go too," Keely said.

Keely looked down. With one hand, she started tracing a pattern in the dirt.

"Mama said her home is here with Miss Leandra. But she wants me to have a chance in the world. And to have that chance, she said I have to leave The Cedars."

Keely looked up and met my eyes. "I—I want to go too," she added. "I want to get an education and a real job. I want to make a place for myself. I want that more than anything."

She paused. "But I don't want to leave you," she finished.

"You've been a wonderful friend, Keely. I couldn't have made it through all these terrible times without you."

Tears came to my eyes. I got a lump in my throat. But I went on firmly.

"But I have my brother now. You have to go. You deserve to go. And you have to go soon—tomorrow. The longer you stay, the harder it will be to leave."

I paused and then added, "And the harder it will be

THE FREEDOM TREE

for me to say good-bye."

"I'll miss you," Keely said shyly.

"I'll miss you more than I can say," I answered truthfully.

Tomorrow Keely would start a new life. So would I. Tomorrow our paths would separate.

But now we clasped hands. We sat together for a last few minutes. We sat under the big oak—black and white, free and equal.

Author's Note

In 1858, Abraham Lincoln made a famous speech. In it he said, "A house divided against itself cannot stand. I believe this government cannot endure . . . half-slave and half-free."

He was right. Two years later he was elected president, and slavery tore the country apart.

The Civil War was fought from 1861 to 1865. The war was between the northern states of the Union and the southern states of the Confederacy. Americans from both the North and South paid a terrible price to save the country and end slavery.

At the end of the war, a Southern farmer said that his state was "almost like a desert." He said there were "no cattle, hogs, sheep, horses, or anything else . . ." He noted that the barns were all burned. Chimneys stood without houses. Houses stood without roofs, doors, or windows.

Entire cities were destroyed in the war. Families were torn apart. More Americans died in the Civil War than in all the other wars our country has fought combined.